Maddie's Story

Written by
Barbara West

Illustrated by
Johannes Christian

For my brave and beautiful aunt, Kay, who has always inspired and encouraged me.

About the author:
Ms. West is an educator with a Master's Degree in English.

Maddie's Story © 2023 Barbara West All rights reserved.
No part of this publication may be reproduced, stored in a retrieval system, or transmitted, in any form, or by any means, electronic, mechanical, photocopying, recording, or otherwise, without the prior consent of the publisher.

Maddie's Story

Written by
Barbara West

Illustrated by
Johannes Christian

Hello! My name is Madison Elaine, but sometimes Mommy calls me Maddie or Pumpkin when I get into trouble, like the time I took more than five rolls of toilet paper from the closet and unrolled them all over the floor in every room: living room, bathroom, bedrooms, and kitchen.

Mommy said, "Maddie, you've been quite mischievous! Why did you do that?" Oops, I got in trouble!

My color is predominantly white with beige patches on my back and ears. I weigh 20 pounds, which is considered to be a medium sized dog.

I came to my forever family from far away, in California – Fresno, I think. I rode on a Greyhound bus, but all the people did not scare me. They wanted to hug and kiss and pet me.

My new family consists of my mommy and my grandmother, who I call Nana. I describe myself as happy, funny, and precocious. I like to play a lot with Mom. I know what time she arrives home from work, so I wait impatiently at the front door until she arrives because I'm anxious to greet her and play. As soon as she walks through the door, I jump up on her, and she gives me kisses and hugs and says, "Maddie, I love you. You are the best puppy in the world. Have you been a good girl today?"

I have a lot of new toys that I enjoy playing with. They are a variety of shapes and colors: red, yellow, blue, green, pink, and white. Some of the shapes are circles, squares, rectangles, and triangles. However, my favorite toy is my red frisbee. Mommy throws it, and I fetch it back to her. Sometimes, though, I stop to play, and Mommy yells, "Maddie!" and I return back to her as rapidly as I can.

Yes, I enjoy playing a lot. Sometimes my Nana forgets and leaves her socks on the bedroom floor. Then, I will rush into the room and grab them quickly and spend a great deal of time searching for a great place to hide them so Nana can't find them. Sometimes she finds them, but often she does not. Sometimes I forget where I hid them, but eventually I find them again, and that makes me HAPPY.

I like it when company comes to visit. When my young cousins visit, they crawl around on the floor and play with me. We have lots of fun. And, once when my aunt came to visit, I ran across the room quite fast and hopped on her lap and sat and watched television. She was very surprised, but she kissed me. Also, once when my mom was pulling her orange laundry bag to the washing machine, I sneaked a ride on the bag. Nana stated that I looked as if I were riding in a convertible car in a parade, and she laughed.

Because I'm such a busy bee most of the time, Nana says I must take a nap during the day. I have three beds. One is very large and grey in color, one is medium size and blue and green, and the final one is small and red. I prefer the largest bed because when I'm in it, I can roll around and around and play. Sometimes I pretend to be outside digging in the dirt, and at other times I burrow down deep in my bed and hide.

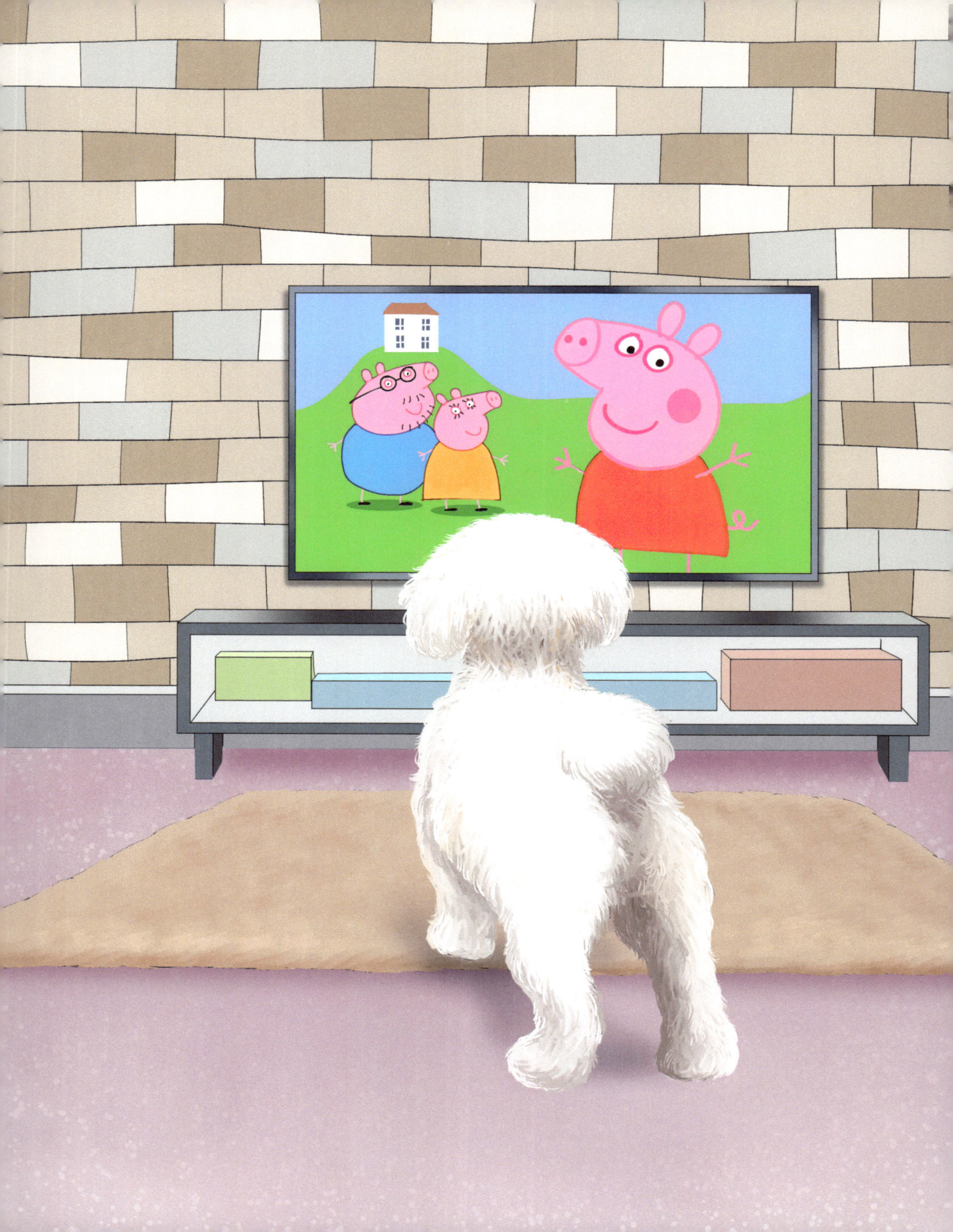

When I was a baby, I did not want to go to bed at night or take a daytime nap. So, Mommy turned the TV on to play classical music, and I fell asleep immediately; it still works. I also like cartoons. Some of my favorites are *Peppa Pig*, *Dora*, *Popeye*, and *Max and Ruby*.

I like people, and they like me. When I go to the vet or the groomer, everyone wants to pet or kiss me. Once, when I broke my leg, I had surgery and needed to stay overnight at the animal hospital. I was scared, but Mommy phoned me during the night, and hearing her voice made me feel better. My doctor was also very nice and compassionate. He took my picture during the night and sent it to Mommy, and she felt reassured and thanked him.

Another way I entertain myself is by sitting in my front door and greeting my neighbors as they pass by. Some are walking their dogs while others are jogging. Some are simply walking alone or with someone else. I bark at them, and they say, "Hello, Madison." The dogs bark back to say hi. Some of the dogs are my special friends. They are Toby, a brown Pug; Lulu, a black and white Poodle; and Buttons, a small Bichon like me.

Because our neighborhood has dangerous coyotes, I cannot go into the backyard without an adult. So, I often use my potty pad. I learned how to use it fast when I was young. As soon as I used it, I would drag it to Mommy or Nana, and then I got a treat. I'm older now; my birthday is in November. I don't drag the potty pad anymore; I just bark once and the adults know what that means.

I recently experienced another adventure when I accidentally closed myself in the bathroom. At first no one missed me, because I did not bark. I just laid down and fell asleep. Soon, though, Mommy found me, and I was GLAD!

Once when I was younger, I heard a very loud noise. BANG! I became frightened, and when Nana opened the door, I ran outside – fast. I ran to the end of the block like when I take walks with Mom, but I did not go into the street, because that's DANGEROUS. Nana and our friend, Miss Jean, came searching for me, and I was joyful to see them and to return home. I'm certainly never doing that again! I still dislike loud noise, so, when Mommy uses the robot vacuum cleaner, I run and hide in my secure place underneath the large chair in my bedroom.

Breakfast is my favorite meal. Mommy cooks me chicken. However, I also eat brown food that is delivered in a colorful bag. Mommy orders it, because the doctor says I need the vitamins it contains in order to grow strong. But I love to eat chicken so much that when Mommy is preparing it, I spin in circles, jump high and stand on my hind legs and beg. And I dance in place. Yes, chicken is my very favorite food! Sometimes when I've eaten all of my chicken, I push my food bowl to where Mom is sitting so she can add more, but she says no, I've had enough.

I LOVE my mommy and Nana. Once when Nana went to the hospital, I missed her very much. I sat at the door and watched and watched for her to come home. I was very SAD. When she came home, I was happy again.

I am a hypoallergenic dog, which means I am good for people who have allergies. However, my veterinarian says I have allergies, so I take an allergy pill daily. Mom wraps it in peanut butter. I like peanut butter, so sometimes I fake sneeze in order to get more, but Mommy will say, "Madison, you're just pretending. No more peanut butter for you today."

Oh, I forgot. Nana says I must exercise so that I will be strong and healthy. And we live near a park with a nature center, so we walk there occasionally. I enjoy walking, because we see a lot of interesting animals playing, birds chirping, and ducks swimming in the pond. There are cute rabbits, playful squirrels, fun looking racoons, and lots of different dogs, big and small. I also see lots of green grass, big trees, and numerous beautiful flowers of all varieties and colors: red, yellow, pink, orange, purple, and more. And while walking to the park, I always obey mom when she says, "Maddie, we must stop and look both ways before crossing the street."

So, my forever home makes me very happy. I love my family and friends, and they love me. If you are ever in my neighborhood, come past my home and I will bark at you to say hi, and you can bark back. Or just say, "Hello, Madison."

Goodbye for now.

Printed in the USA
CPSIA information can be obtained
at www.ICGtesting.com
LVHW060341161123
764090LV00013B/62